KUNG FU PANDA
LEGENDS OF AWESOMENESS™
nickelodeon™

MASTER OF MANNERS

adapted by Tina Gallo

Simon Spotlight
New York London Toronto Sydney New Delhi

Dominick

SIMON SPOTLIGHT
An imprint of Simon & Schuster Children's Publishing Division
1230 Avenue of the Americas, New York, New York 10020
This Simon Spotlight paperback edition May 2016
Kung Fu Panda: Legends of Awesomeness © 2016 Viacom International Inc. All Rights Reserved. NICKELODEON
and all related logos are trademarks of Viacom International Inc. "Kung Fu Panda" © 2008 DreamWorks Animation LLC.
All Rights Reserved. All rights reserved including the right of reproduction in whole or in part in any form.
SIMON SPOTLIGHT and colophon are registered trademarks of Simon & Schuster, Inc.
For information about special discounts for bulk purposes please contact Simon & Schuster Special Sales
at 1-866-506-1949 or business@simonandschuster.com.
Manufactured in the United States of America 0416 LAK
2 4 6 8 10 9 7 5 3 1
ISBN 978-1-4814-6183-2
ISBN 978-1-4814-6184-9 (eBook)

The Furious Five were just sitting down to lunch. Po had been fighting with Temutai but let him get away. Master Shifu was disappointed. "You let Temutai get away?" he asked Po.

Po had a mouthful of food, but that didn't stop him from answering Master Shifu. "Of course I didn't let him get away," he said. Everyone looked at Po in disgust as he kept chewing and talking. "Well, maybe I let him get away. But it's not going to happen again! Next time I see Temutai, he's mine!" Po noticed a mooncake on a plate. "And so is that mooncake!" He grabbed it and popped it in his mouth.

"Hey!" Monkey said, annoyed.

"Oh, I'm sorry," Po said. "Did you want that?" He spit the mooncake out of his mouth and into his hand. He offered it to Monkey.

"Forget it," Monkey said.

It was just then that Constable Hu showed up. "I have exciting news!" he told the Furious Five. "Upper Head District Chief Superior Superintendent Chang is going to be passing through our village. I'm going to throw him a banquet."

Po was excited. "A banquet!" he shouted. "I've always wanted to go to one."

But Master Shifu did not share Po's enthusiasm.

"I'm sorry, Constable Hu. We don't attend banquets for bureaucrats," he said with a sniff.

Constable Hu was upset. "Oh, but please come! I need you! If you don't come, he may not approve my transfer!"

Master Shifu suddenly looked interested. "Your *transfer*?" he said. "Who said we're not coming?! Of *course* we're coming!"

Po raised his hands in the air in celebration. "Wooo! Yeah! Par-tay! Wooo!"

Master Shifu looked at Constable Hu and smiled. "We could even do a performance at the banquet if you like."

Constable Hu was touched by Master Shifu's offer. "Thank you! I can't tell you how much this means to me! This banquet shall be the most sophisticated, elegant . . ."

Po spilled some milk and started licking it off the table. Then he spit it back into his cup. Tigress watched him in disgust.

Constable Hu was startled by Po's bad manners. "As I was saying, it will be the most dignified soiree the valley has even seen." He gave Po a nervous look before he left.

Master Shifu smiled dreamily. "If this banquet goes well, Constable Hu will be leaving us. No more of his permits . . . his endless forms . . . his constant meddling. We'll be free!"

A couple of days later Crane asked Master Shifu about the banquet. "What time should we start heading down to the banquet?"

"I believe the invitation said it started at six," Master Shifu said. "So . . ."

Po looked confused. "Wait. Constable Hu sent you your invitation? You got it?"

Master Shifu looked surprised. "Of course he did. We all got them."

"Didn't you get yours?" Monkey asked.

"Huh," Po replied. He was too embarrassed to say he hadn't received an invitation. He decided to go to Constable Hu's office and speak with him. Constable Hu greeted Po with a big fake smile.

"Constable Hu, there seems to be a problem with my invitation," Po said. "I didn't actually get it. Yet."

"Didn't get it? Really?" Constable Hu said. "Well, that's odd. Oh, I remember now. You're not invited."

Po was shocked. "Why not?"

"Oh, Po, I feel terrible about this," Constable Hu said. "But your manners—they're atrocious! I'm sorry, but I can't expose Chang to that! You know how important this night is to me."

Po returned to the Jade Palace and told everyone what Constable Hu said.

"Do you guys think the way I eat is disgusting?" Po asked.

"We try not to watch," Mantis said.

"Only because it's too disgusting," Crane added.

"I understand," Po said. I'm gross and disgusting and nobody wants to be around me. Now, if you'll excuse me, I'll be in my room hiding my hideousness."

Meanwhile, Temutai was waiting for his invitation to the banquet too. He asked one of his warriors to find out what happened to it.

The Buffalo Warrior gulped. "I'm sorry, Temutai. But . . . you're not invited."

"What!" Temutai roared. "Do you know how that makes me feel? To be the only one who isn't going?"

"Oh, but you're not!" the Buffalo Warrior said. "The Dragon Warrior hasn't been invited either!"

At first Temutai was surprised. But then he thought about Po. "That makes sense. I've seen the way he eats."

But then Temutai brightened. "If the Dragon Warrior is not there, our mission will be that much easier! Prepare the troops! Gather all the weapons! If I can't enjoy that banquet, no one will!"

Meanwhile, back at the Jade Palace, Po had locked himself in his room. But Master Shifu insisted on seeing him.

"Po, open this door," Master Shifu ordered.

Po opened the door—and handed Master Shifu a blindfold.

"Here's a blindfold so you don't have to gaze upon my grossness," he said. "You know, when I was a kid, I didn't get invited to banquets for the same reason. But I'd hide in a pot and watch. And I'd say to myself, 'One day that's going to be me sitting there, having a good banquety time. One day I'm going to be invited to one of these things.' Looks like I was wrong."

But Master Shifu had a surprise for Po.

"Po, I just wanted to let you know that we'll be leaving for the banquet in an hour," Master Shifu said.

"Have a good time," Po said bitterly.

"I plan to—because you're coming with us!" Master Shifu said.

Po couldn't believe his ears.

"What? Really?" he said.

"I taught you the secrets of kung fu," Master Shifu said. "I can certainly teach you manners. Now, in order to identify which of your manners needs improvement, I need to watch you eat."

But after watching Po eat, Master Shifu realized he had met his match. It would take more than an hour to teach Po good table manners. Po would have to stay home.

"I'm sorry, Po. I failed you," Master Shifu said.

"No, I failed you guys," Po said sadly. "I'm not worthy of a fancy banquet." Everyone felt bad for Po.

"You gonna be okay?" Monkey asked.

Po sighed. "Yeah. I'll be fine," he said.

Meanwhile, at the banquet, Constable Hu was a nervous wreck. Even though everything was beautiful, Superintendent Chang was not having a good time. Constable Hu hoped a performance by the Furious Five would put him in a better mood.

"The fun is just about to begin, right, Master Shifu?" Constable Hu said.

"Yes, certainly," Master Shifu said. "The Furious Five will now perform a display of skill and daring—the Pinnacle of Perfection!"

Superintendent Chang shocked everyone by letting out a loud belch. "Seen it!" he said. "Every kung fu palace I visit does the Pinnacle of Perfection."

"Oh," Master Shifu said. "What about the Flaming . . ."

"Boring!" Superintendent Chang yelled. "Do something else!"

Before Master Shifu could suggest anything else, Temutai broke in.

"Sorry to break in," Temutai said. "I forgot my invitation. No, wait. I didn't get one!" Temutai and his team immediately attacked the Furious Five.

Meanwhile, Po decided to sneak into the party in a barrel, just the way he used to do as a child.

Temutai stood in front of him and blocked his path.

"Temutai got an invite and I didn't?" Po said, shocked.

Then he looked around and realized Temutai was there to fight the Furious Five.

Temutai laughed at Po. "You at a banquet? You'd never fit in. You're a slob. And you have no manners!"

"Temutai, I'm going to make you eat, silently chew, and then politely swallow those words," Po said.

Po and Temutai fought. And as they fought, Po suddenly remembered the good manners he'd been trying to learn his entire life.

"Elbows off the table," Po said. "Mustn't slouch. No talking with your mouth full. And no spitting, either!"

Temutai tried to fight back, but he was no match for Po. "I apologize," Temutai said. "You have excellent manners," he told Po just before he passed out.

Constable Hu thanked Po. "Thanks ever so much, Dragon Warrior!" he said nervously. "Now . . . skedaddle, and here's a cookie for your trouble."

Po was just about to leave when Superintendent Chang stood up.

"Wait!" he said. "This warrior deserves a place at our table."

Po walked to the banquet table, beaming.

"Now we eat," Superintendent Chang said.

Po was seated right next to the superintendent!

Superintendent Chang and Po were both served a large plate of dumplings. Po immediately dropped one on the floor. Everyone gasped!

Po was mortified. Would he have to leave the banquet?

But the superintendent picked the dumpling up off the floor and smiled as he popped it in his mouth!

Everyone gasped again! His manners were as bad as Po's!

"Here comes the wagon!" the superintendent said cheerfully, and let out a loud belch!

"I'm right with you!" Po shouted.

Master Shifu chuckled. "Well, this evening is a success. Constable Hu should be promoted and sent away at once!"

Superintendent Chang shook his head. "I couldn't do that to you, Huey!" he said. "This place is great. I'm going to renew your post for another year. Heck, let's make it ten!"

"Here comes the wagon again!" Po shouted. He took a deep breath and got ready to let out a huge belch.

"Wait for me!" Superintendent Chang yelled.

"Nooo!" everyone else shouted.

Po knew he'd have to use good manners if he ever wanted to be invited to a banquet again. But not today!